To
Reggie, Izzie, Madaket, Lilly,
Bella, Sheldon, Cookie,
Ladybug, Darby, and Teddy.

First edition April 2018. Print and E-book design and formatting by Mike Quinones G.

The Perfect Pet
The Adventures and Misadventures of Nissa
The Youngest Woodland Fairy Who Always Speaks in Verse

To Mrs H
classroom!

BB Walsh

WRITTEN BY BB WALSH
ILLUSTRATED BY MIKE QUINONES G

Every morning while sprinkling fairy dust, Nissa watched a lady walk her dog in the park. They played fetch and gave each other lots of hugs and kisses.

"I'd love to have a pet one day, one who will love me, hug and play."

"Pets are wonderful and fun, but they're a lot of work, too,"
Darla the Dragonfly said.

"I know they'll need some special care.
I'll feed them well and wash their hair.
But how hard could it really be
if I love them and they love me? "

"What kind of pet
would you like?"
Darla asked.

"How 'bout an ant? Or other bug?
They've lots of arms for lots of hugs."

Darla and Nissa fluttered around the woodlands to find the perfect pet.
They spotted a line of marching ants.

"Hi, Mr. Ant. Now that we've met,
would you like to be my pet?
I'll rub your tummy when you stretch.
We'll go for walks and play some fetch."

Mr. Ant looked from Nissa to Darla.

"Fetch, Mr. Ant."
Darla picked up a small pebble and threw it.

Mr. Ant scuttled off, picked up the
pebble, and joined a line of other ants marching into the woods.

Darla shook her head.
"That's not how to play fetch."

Nissa and Darla flittered up through the trees and spotted a
caterpillar chomping on a green leaf.

"Miss Caterpillar, would you let
me love you like a family pet?
I'll rub your tummy when you stretch.
We'll go for walks and play some fetch."

Miss Caterpillar smiled at Nissa.

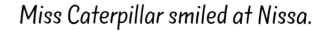

"Would you like to go for a walk?" Darla asked.

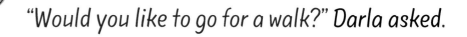

"I'll be right down and meet you on the forest floor," said Miss Caterpillar.

YUM! YUM!

Darla and Nissa flew to the ground and waited...

and waited...

and waited...

and waited...

and waited...

for Miss Caterpillar to come down and join them.

As they waited, a mouse hurried past them.

"Please stop, Miss Mouse, and don't you fret,
I'd like for you to be my pet.
I'll rub your tummy when you stretch.
We'll go for walks and play some fetch."

Miss Mouse's nose wiggled as she sniffed Darla.
Her whiskers quivered as she sniffed Nissa.

Darla threw a pebble.
Miss Mouse scurried, picked it up, and returned the pebble to Darla.

Nissa and Darla walked with Miss Mouse
all the way back to Nissa's house.

They laughed as they played fetch with Miss Mouse.

Nissa combed Miss Mouse's soft honey-brown hair as
Miss Mouse ate berries and seeds.

"She's so cute, and she's so soft,
and she can sleep up in my loft."

"I'm so happy. I just bet
that she will make the perfect pet."

"Because she's sweet, and brown, and funny
I think I'd like to name her Honey."

"I'll say goodbye now. I hope you have a
nice quiet night with your new pet,"
Darla said.

Up in her loft, Nissa tucked Honey
under a warm, blue blanket at the foot of her bed.

Nissa
fell fast asleep
and dreamed about
all the fun adventures she and
Honey would have together.

They would hike the trails up a mountainside.
They would cool off in the lake on a sunny day.

They would chase each other and play fetch in the park.

In the morning, Nissa woke up and stretched. She stepped from her bed and tripped over the blue blanket.

"Honey! Honey, where are you? We've got lots of things to do."

Nissa's house was a mess. Jars of nectar were tipped over and all her sweets were missing.

"Where are you, Honey?
This mess isn't funny."

She flittered out her front door calling,

"Honey.
Oh, Honey!
I'll get down on one knee
and beg you to come home.
You'll get lost if you roam.

Oh Honey,
my Honey.
Please, come back to me."

"What's wrong, Nissa? Where's Honey?" Darla asked.

"I don't know, I'm not sure.
What a mess she has made.
I was sleeping, heard nothing.
She's gone, I'm afraid.

I warmed up fruit nectar,
and she mostly drank it.
Then gave her a hug and a nice,
warm, blue blanket.
We both settled in and fell fast asleep,
Then she made that big mess without even a peep."

"I'm not surprised. My mother told me that mice don't sleep much at
night because they go looking for food," Darla said.

"It's not your fault, Nissa. Honey was just here for a visit. I'm sure she's home by now. We should have learned more about mice before you asked Honey to be your pet," Darla said.

"We should have asked questions,

or asked for advice,

and learned what we could 'bout

ants, caterpillars, and mice.

But before I decide on which pet to posses,

I confess I'm not eager to clean up this mess.

As for the next pet, I will just wait and see...

I think I will wait for that pet to find me."

THE END

*Draw a picture of you and your pet and
post it on Facebook. #NissaPERFECTPET*

Books by BB Walsh

The Adventures and Misadventures
of Nissa the Woodland Fairy Series
Bullies Be Gone
The Perfect Pet
Nissa to the Rescue
Too Many Talents
The Not So Lucky Charm
Daisey's Bright Birthday
Pixie Problems
A Little Help, Helps a Lot
Nissa Tells a Tale
The Best Christmas Tree Ever

COLOR ME!!!!!

Made in the USA
Middletown, DE
12 January 2019